Christn Instrumental Solos
Carols & Traditional Classics

Produced by
Alfred Music Publishing Co., Inc.
P.O. Box 10003
Van Nuys, CA 91410-0003
alfred.com

Printed in USA.

GESÙ BAMBINO
(The Infant Jesus)

English Words by FREDERICK H. MARTENS
Music and Original Lyrics PIETRO A. YON

CAROL MEDLEY

(Hark! The Herald Angels Sing/O Come, All Ye Faithful/The First Noel)

Moderately (♩ = 104)

"Hark! The Herald Angels Sing"
Words by CHARLES WESLEY
Music by FELIX MENDELSSOHN

"O Come, All Ye Faithful"
(Adeste Fideles)
English Words by FREDERICK OAKELEY
Latin Words Attributed to JOHN FRANCIS WADE
Music by JOHN READING

Carol Medley - 2 - 1
IFM0227CD

O HOLY NIGHT
(Cantique de Noel)

Music by ADOLPHE CHARLES ADAM
Words by JOHN SULLIVAN DWIGHT

Slowly, with expression (♩. = 66)

IFM0227CD

ANGELS MEDLEY
(Angels from the Realms of Glory/Angels We Have Heard on High)

Angels from the Realms of Glory
Words by JAMES MONTGOMERY
Music by HENRY SMART

IFM0227CD

Themes from
THE NUTCRACKER SUITE

Music by
PETER ILYICH TCHAIKOVSKY

Themes From the Nutcracker Suite - 6 - 1
IFM0227CD

March

Themes From the Nutcracker Suite - 6 - 2
IFM0227CD

Dance of the Sugar-Plum Fairy

Russian Dance (Trepak)

*An easier alternative note has been provided.

**E♯ = F♮

Waltz of the Flowers

Bright waltz, in one (♩. = 60)

*B♯ = C♮
**E♯ = F♮

LO, HOW A ROSE E'ER BLOOMING

Harmonized by MICHAEL PRAETORIUS

IFM0227CD

MANGER MEDLEY
(Away in a Manger (Cradle Song)/Away in a Manger/Silent Night)

Moderately (♩ = 84)

Away in a Manger (Cradle Song)
Music by WILLIAM JAMES KIRKPATRICK

Away in a Manger
TRADITIONAL

Silent Night
English Words adapted from the original German of JOSEPH MOHR
Music by FRANZ GRUBER

IFM0227CD

FOLK CAROL SUITE
I. Noël Nouvelet

FRENCH CAROL

II. Masters In This Hall

ENGLISH CAROL

Folk Carol Suite - 5 - 2
IFM0227CD

III. Coventry Carol
(Lullay, Thou Little Tiny Child)

ENGLISH CAROL

IV. O Du Fröhliche/Echo Carol

GERMAN CAROLS

Folk Carol Suite - 5 - 4
IFM0227CD

INFANT HOLY, INFANT LOWLY

POLISH CAROL

IFM0227CD

CELEBRATION MEDLEY
(Hallelujah Chorus/Joy to the World)

Majestically (♩ = 88)
Hallelujah Chorus
Music by GEORGE FREDERICK HANDEL

Joy to the World
Words by ISAAC WATTS
Music by GEORGE F. HANDEL

Celebration Medley - 2 - 1
IFM0227CD

PARTS OF A CLARINET AND FINGERING CHART

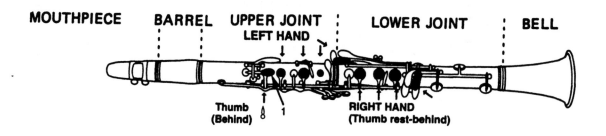

● = press the key or cover the hole with your finger.
○ = do not press the key or cover the hole.

When there is more than one fingering given for a note, use the first one unless the alternate fingering is suggested.

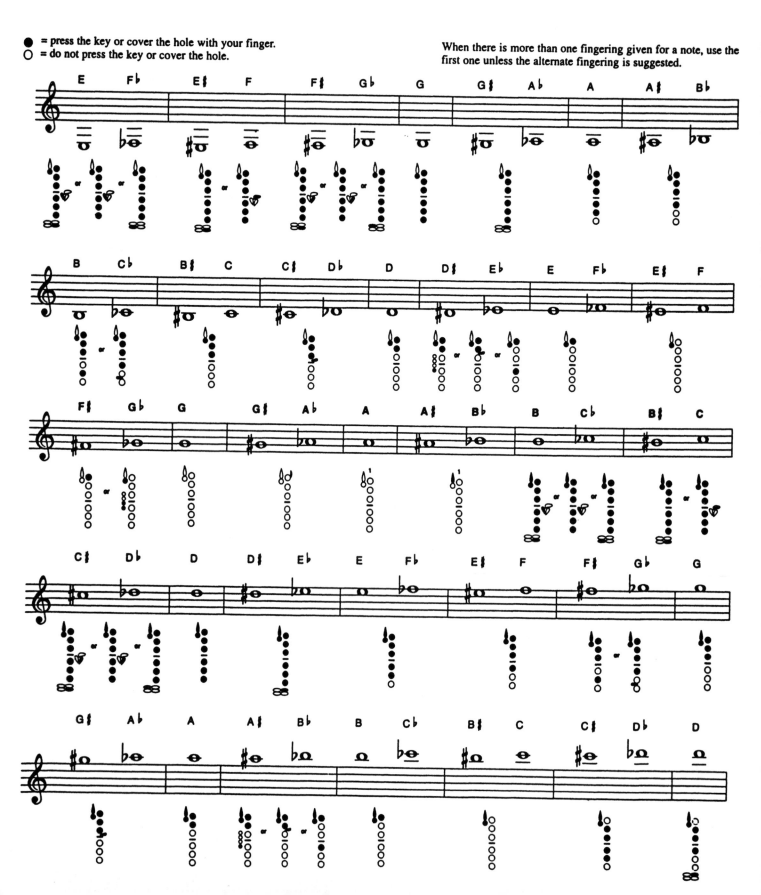